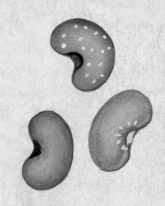
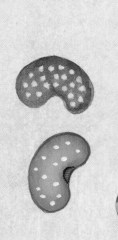

# *The* GIANT
## AND THE BEANSTALK

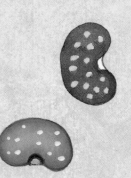

# WRITTEN AND ILLUSTRATED
# BY DIANE STANLEY

HarperCollins*Publishers*

**O**nce there was a giant named Otto. He lived with his family in a magical kingdom high above the troubles and cares of the human world below.

Otto was big, of course, with razor-sharp teeth and beady little eyes. His hands and feet were enormous, with long, menacing claws. He looked, in other words, like your typical fierce, ferocious young giant.

Only he wasn't.

He was embarrassingly polite. At school he never made above a *C-* in Cursing, Growling, or Stomping (he would have made all *D*s except that his teachers worried about his self-esteem). And he didn't see the point of smashing things with clubs and boulders. Then, as if all that weren't bad enough, there was the matter of Otto's pet.

His parents, who thought every young giant should have something to love and care for, offered to buy him whichever pet he wanted. They hoped he would choose something fierce—a werewolf or a baby dragon. Not Otto! He came home with . . . a hen.

All right, it was a special hen that could lay golden eggs—but still! The other giants couldn't stop laughing. Otto didn't care. He thought Clara (for that was her name) was the softest, sweetest creature he had ever seen. And he loved her dearly.

One morning Otto was awakened by a suspicious noise. His parents had gone out early, so he and Clara were alone. Otto slipped out of bed and padded barefoot down the hall to investigate. There, right in the middle of his living room, was an honest-to-goodness human!

Otto couldn't believe it! Humans lived down below. They never came up to the Kingdom of Giants. But it was a human all right, no doubt about that. Otto had seen pictures of them in his Social Studies book.

Just then Clara, who had been sleeping sweetly, awoke with a soft little cackle. The human grabbed her and popped her into his sack. It was the single worst moment in Otto's life.

He had to do something! He took a deep breath and ran into the room, shouting the scariest thing he could remember from fourth-grade Threats and Curses:

"Fee, fi, fo, fum,
I smell the blood of an Englishman!
Be he alive or be he dead,
I'll grind his bones to make my bread!"

The thief let out a terrible shriek and went dashing out the door as fast as his skinny little legs could go—taking Clara with him! In less time than it takes to tell it, the human was over the edge of the kingdom and climbing down, down, down . . . what was it? It was . . . a *beanstalk!*

Otto was terrified of heights, but this was an emergency. He got a firm grip on the beanstalk and began the long climb down.

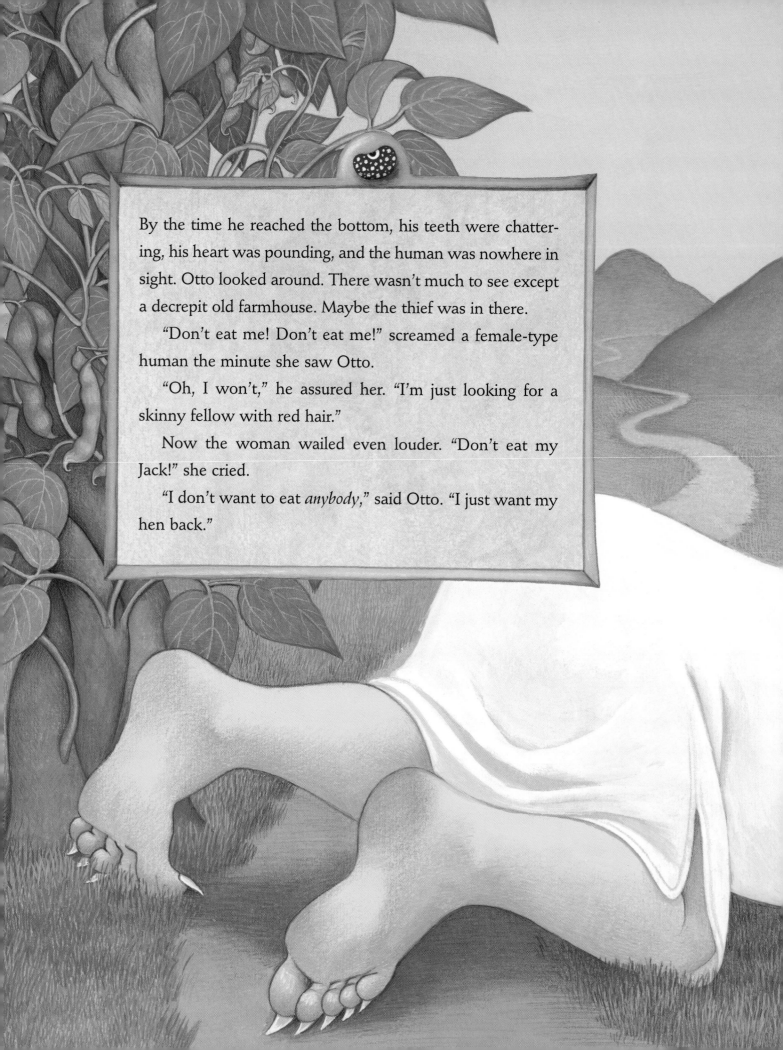

By the time he reached the bottom, his teeth were chattering, his heart was pounding, and the human was nowhere in sight. Otto looked around. There wasn't much to see except a decrepit old farmhouse. Maybe the thief was in there.

"Don't eat me! Don't eat me!" screamed a female-type human the minute she saw Otto.

"Oh, I won't," he assured her. "I'm just looking for a skinny fellow with red hair."

Now the woman wailed even louder. "Don't eat my Jack!" she cried.

"I don't want to eat *anybody*," said Otto. "I just want my hen back."

"Oh," said the woman, a little calmer now. "That was yours? The magical hen that lays golden eggs? I'm afraid my boy has gone off to sell her. She's worth a fortune."

"Oh, no!" cried Otto.

"I'm so sorry," she said. "It's just that he wanted to get the money to buy back our old cow, Milky White—a worthless creature, really. But my Jack loves her like anything! He used to *sing* to her while he did the milking—*imagine!* And she'd join in for the chorus: *Moo, moo, moo.* Well, when she stopped giving milk, we had to sell her, and Jack just wasn't the same after that. He's not a thief, really. He just did it for love of the cow."

"I believe you," said Otto. "And you can keep the golden egg. But I have to get my hen back."

"Of course you do," the woman said. "You shouldn't have any trouble finding my boy. Just ask for Jack."

Like all male giants, Otto hated asking directions. It was so embarrassing! But what else could he do?

Naturally, he ran into problems with the very first person he met. Before Otto could utter a word, the fellow ran for his life and scurried up a nearby tree. (This put him right at eye level for a giant, but nobody ever said humans were smart.) Otto asked where he might find Jack.

The fellow pointed a trembling finger. "That house there," he said.

Otto thanked the man politely, then hurried over and knocked on the door.

It was opened by a human with curly black hair. This wasn't Jack!

One look at Otto and the man turned and fled—leaping nimbly over a table as he went, over the candlestick that was on it, and, quick as a flash, escaping through an open window.

It was beginning to dawn on Otto that scaring humans, while kind of exciting, made his search a whole lot harder. So he stopped in a meadow and wove a flower crown. Then he pulled out his pocketknife and trimmed his claws.

Sure enough, the next person Otto met looked a little wary but didn't run away. "Yes, I know Jack," the man said. "That's him up there on the hill, with his sister."

Otto squinted suspiciously at the two figures.
They seemed awfully small, and neither of them
had red hair. Suddenly he heard a scream, and the
boy tumbled down the hill, landing with a thump
at Otto's feet.

"Ow!" he groaned. "My head!"

Seconds later, his sister landed on top of him.
"Ow!" the boy said again.

Otto helped them to their feet, then headed
on down the road. "Wrong again," he muttered to
himself. "That wasn't Jack, either."

The next "Jack" he was directed to was a regular beanpole of a man. Otto found him out in the backyard, cooking on a charcoal grill.

"Sprat's the name," he said. "How can I help you?"

"I'm afraid you can't," said Otto with a sigh. "I'm looking for a red-headed fellow named Jack, and nobody seems to know where he is."

Mr. Sprat turned to his plump and rosy wife. "Dearest, isn't there a red-headed Jack just down the way?"

"Indeed there is," she agreed, smiling sweetly up at Otto. "Not far at all. But can't we give you something to nibble on? A nice steak and butter sandwich, perhaps?"

"Or some lovely grilled celery?" called the man as Otto hurried away.

Finally, in a little house about half a mile from the Sprats', Otto found a human with red hair. But of course it wasn't Jack—just a little boy who was gobbling down an entire Christmas pie without benefit of fork, spoon, napkin, or plate. It was a terrible mess.

"Keeps him out of trouble," said the boy's mother. Then she smiled and started to close the door.

"Wait!" cried Otto. "Please help me! I've been looking and *looking* for a human named Jack. He has red hair and he stole my hen and plans to sell her so he can buy back his old cow!"

"Oh, well—why didn't you say so before?" said the woman. "Go to the market town. That's where people buy and sell things. You're sure to find him there."

Otto had reached the outskirts of town when he heard a voice calling, "Jack!" Finally! he thought. But all he saw was a young lady, all forlorn, clutching a pail and frowning at an old cow with a crumpled horn.

"Be right there!" came a voice from the far side of the house. There was a rip and a thump. After a minute a young fellow appeared. His clothes were all tattered and torn and he was limping. "Fell off the ladder," he explained. "Caught on a nail," he added. Naturally, it wasn't Jack.

"Just look at this cow you bought," cried the lady. "She won't give milk! Not a drop!"

Ah-ha! thought Otto. It's the wrong human but the right cow! He walked over to the couple. "Excuse me," he said, "but did you buy that cow from a red-haired fellow?"

"I did, and it was a big mistake. I traded some genuine magic beans for her and turns out she's dry as a bone."

Otto bought the cow on the spot. Then he picked her up and carried her into town.

Which is where Otto found Jack. The real Jack. Red-headed Jack. He had a hen in his lap. Jack hadn't had the heart to sell Clara after all!

"*Mooo!*" lowed Milky White the minute she saw Jack.

"*Cluck, cluck, cluck!*" cackled Clara as soon as she saw Otto.

Jack looked up in surprise.

"Want to trade?" Otto said.

So they did.

Once Otto and Clara were safely back in the Kingdom of
Giants, Jack cut down the beanstalk. He collected enough
beans from it to make soup every day for the rest of his life.
But he and his mother soon got tired of bean soup, so they
opened a roadside stand to sell Jack 'n' Ma's Homemade
Soup Mix. It was a great success.

With the proceeds from the sale of the golden egg, they fixed up the house and bought a new cow (one that actually gave milk) to keep Milky White company. And you'll be glad to know that Jack's mother was right—he really was a good boy, and he never stole anything again.

As for Otto, he was a hero for rescuing Clara from the human. Soon all the giants were wearing flower crowns and trimming their nails. Poetry was taught in the schools, instead of curses. Being fierce went completely out of style.

Otto is now invited to everybody's parties, and usually he goes. But he is still happiest when he is alone with Clara, sitting in the garden and smelling the roses. Sometimes in the afternoons, if the wind is blowing just right, they can hear the distant sound of music drifting up from the human world below—a charming melody, sung in a fine baritone voice, with a strange chorus. It sounds like a human and a cow—or is it *two* cows?

And it always makes Otto smile.

Jack be nimble, Jack be quick,
Jack jump over the candlestick.

Jack and Jill went up the hill
To fetch a pail of water.
Jack fell down and broke his crown,
And Jill went tumbling after.

Jack Sprat could eat no fat.
His wife could eat no lean.
And 'twixt them both
they cleared the cloth
and licked the platter clean.

Little Jack Horner
Sat in a corner
Eating a Christmas pie.
He put in his thumb
And pulled out a plum
And said,
"What a good boy am I!"

This is the farmer sowing the corn,
That kept the cock that crowed in the morn,
That waked the priest all shaven and shorn,
That married the man all tattered and torn,
That kissed the maiden all forlorn,
That milked the cow with the crumpled horn,
That tossed the dog,
That worried the cat,
That killed the rat,
That ate the malt,
That lay in the house that Jack built.

*For Meredith, of course*

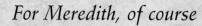

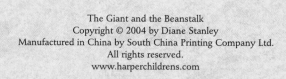

The Giant and the Beanstalk
Copyright © 2004 by Diane Stanley
Manufactured in China by South China Printing Company Ltd.
All rights reserved.
www.harperchildrens.com

Library of Congress Cataloging in Publication Data
Stanley, Diane.
The Giant and the beanstalk / written and illustrated by Diane Stanley.— 1st ed.
p.   cm.
Summary: In this version of the traditional tale, a young giant chases
Jack down the beanstalk to rescue his beloved hen and
meets other Jacks from various nursery rhymes along the way.
ISBN 0-06-000010-4. — ISBN 0-06-000011-2 (lib. bdg.)
[1. Giants—Fiction.  2. Characters from literature—Fiction.]  I. Title.
PZ7.S7869Gi 2004    [E]—dc21
2003001818    CIP
AC
Design by Stephanie Bart-Horvath
1 2 3 4 5 6 7 8 9 10
❖
First Edition